DEAD SCARED

Titles in Teen Reads:

BILLY BUTTON CAVAN SCOTT	**PEST CONTROL** CAVAN SCOTT
DAWN OF THE DAVES TIM COLLINS	**SITTING TARGET** JOHN TOWNSEND
DEAD SCARED TOMMY DONBAVAND	**STALKER** TONY LEE
DEADLY MISSION MARK WRIGHT	**THE HUNTED** CAVAN SCOTT
FAIR GAME ALAN DURANT	**THE CORRIDOR** MARK WRIGHT
JIGSAW LADY TONY LEE	**TROLL** TIM COLLINS
HOME TOMMY DONBAVAND	**UNDERWORLD** SIMON CHESHIRE
KIDNAP TOMMY DONBAVAND	**WARD 13** TOMMY DONBAVAND
MAMA BARKFINGERS CAVAN SCOTT	**WORLD WITHOUT WORDS** JONNY ZUCKER

Badger Publishing Limited, Oldmedow Road, Hardwick Industrial Estate, King's Lynn PE30 4JJ
Telephone: 01438 791037

www.badgerlearning.co.uk

DEAD SCARED

TOMMY DONBAVAND

Dead Scared ISBN 978-1-78147-801-1

Text © Tommy Donbavand 2014
Complete work © Badger Publishing Limited 2014

Publisher: Susan Ross
Senior Editor: Danny Pearson
Publishing Assistant: Claire Morgan
Copyeditor: Cheryl Lanyon
Designer: Bigtop Design Ltd

2 4 6 8 10 9 7 5 3 1

CHAPTER 1

GARY

I was with my mum when she died. Sitting at the side of her hospital bed with the rest of my family – the very same hospital she used to work in. We took turns holding her hand as we watched the blips on her heart and oxygen monitors slowly reducing. Then, with one final, exaggerated breath – almost a last gasp at clinging on to life – she was gone. The lines on the screen were all flat. And the only thing I could think about, after all these months of failing chemotherapy sessions, of watching her grow weaker and weaker as the cancer ate away at her, was that the first dead body I'd ever seen was my own mum's.

The next time I saw my mum, she was in her coffin. It was the morning of her funeral. I had a new suit and stood patiently while my sister tacked up the slightly-too-long trouser legs before my older brother drove me up to the funeral home. He'd been in to visit earlier in the week, but I couldn't bear to go with him. I can't say why. Too upset? Too scared? Who knows? What I did know was that this was my last chance to see her face, so I pushed away the gnawing sensation in my stomach and sat silently in the passenger seat as Ben parked the car.

"Toby," he said, "she's… she's not how you remember her."

"What do you mean?"

"Mum doesn't look like Mum any more. The undertaker said it's because the muscles in your face relax after… you know… so she looks a little different."

I felt like jumping out of the car and running

away there and then. This shouldn't be happening to me. I was only fifteen. Kids don't lose one of their parents while they're still teenagers. Not when they still need them so much. That's all stuff that's supposed to happen way off in the future. The gnawing in my stomach quickly returned.

Ben kept his hand on my shoulder right up until I stepped into the room. And there it was: a polished wooden coffin with the body of my mum inside. I realised that I was trembling. Nervous to be alone with my own mother.

The funeral director had dressed my mum in a pale blue outfit, like a kind of nightdress. And he'd tied a white ribbon in her hair. That made me smile. He didn't have to do that. It was kind.

Ben was right. My mum didn't look quite like herself, but nothing near as different as I had been expecting. I backed away from the coffin and stood at the far end of the room so that I could just see her profile rising up above the wooden casket. That was better. Now she looked like my mum again. And that's when I lost it.

Everything just hit me at once. All the memories, the happy times – and the bad ones. If there was one thing you could say about my mum it's that she had quite a temper. When we fell out, we really fell out. The arguments could last for days. But we always made up. She was my mum, after all.

I suddenly wanted to say sorry for everything I'd ever done to upset or annoy her. All the stupid stuff like staying out all night and not calling, or throwing eggs at our old headteacher's house at Halloween. Pointless, selfish stuff that I'd done thinking that she'd always be there to clean up the mess for me. That she'd be there for her patients at the hospital. That she'd be there forever.

Tears were streaming down my face now. I reached into my pocket for the tissues my sister had given me and pulled out a photograph along with them. It was a snap of me and my mum backstage at last year's school play. I'd been given the lead part and would never forget how, as the curtain rose, I instantly spotted my mum and dad sitting in the middle of the audience. My mum waved to me, even though she knew I couldn't wave back. They'd been so proud of me that night.

Stepping back up to the coffin, I tucked the photograph into my mum's hand, kissed her ice-cold cheek and whispered, "Thank you for everything." Ben's hand reappeared on my shoulder, giving it a squeeze. And then we left.

The funeral itself went without incident. The whole family was there: all the aunts, uncles and cousins we hadn't seen in years – and even some of my mum's cousins from Ireland flew over to be with us. The funeral was, I don't know… nice. There isn't really another word I can use to describe it. My sister had prepared something to say (I was terrified they would ask me as I was considered to be the 'actor' in the family), and I stood at the front of the church with her and my brother as she talked about my mum. How kind she had been, what a fiery temperament she'd had, how brave she'd been in dealing with her illness.

And then I'd laughed out loud. A random memory just popped into my head. Me and my mum had been out shopping when she'd spotted a doormat that had written on it: 'Wipe your feet, stupid!' My mum had always had a good sense of humour, but that doormat just cracked her up. She was literally crying with laughter. I bought it for her out of my pocket money and we giggled all the way home.

Before long, I was standing at the edge of a grave, watching as my mum's coffin was lowered into the ground. My cousin handed me a piece of chewing gum and I popped it into my mouth, biting down hard to try and keep myself from losing it completely. I remember spotting some bloke sitting in a mini digger at the far end of the cemetery, presumably waiting to fill the hole in after we'd finished crying and had left. The day-to-day business of dying, I guess.

We went to a local pub for sandwiches and drinks. I hopped from table to table, glass of coke clutched in my hand, talking to friends and family. For some reason, I felt as though I had to play the host and represent my family. My dad stayed in one place, accepting good wishes from all and sundry, and my brother and sister had their own families to look after. God knows what my little nieces and nephews had made of today.

That's the only reason I sat down with Uncle Gary, my mum's step-brother. I only ever saw him and his family at Christmas if I could help it, nowadays, but my mum had made the effort to visit them at least once a fortnight. She always said that family was the most important thing in the world, and she didn't mind driving twenty-five miles in each direction for a cup of tea and a chat.

It used to annoy my dad that they never visited us instead, that my mum had to do all the running around. But there was little chance of Gary's lot slumming it down to the estate where we lived. Whatever would his millionaire football-player neighbours say if he was seen around our way?

Personally, I could have done without Uncle Gary's boasts about his new car, or holiday villa, or whatever else he'd been spending his money on, but today was all about my mum, and I was determined to do the decent thing and include everyone who'd come to her funeral – no matter how much of an idiot.

Gary had a bunch of empty pint glasses in front of him, and was busy downing another lager when I joined the group. His wife, Anna, sat quietly as ever, wrapped in a white fur coat and nursing a ginger ale. My cousin Mel gave me a smile as I sat down.

"Are you OK?" she asked.

I nodded. "Yeah," I said, "I'm fine." And, to be honest, I was. "It's a bit of a relief, actually. All those months sitting in hospital waiting rooms. My dad bought me a new phone so I could play games like Mad Cats to pass the time, but it didn't really help." It hadn't really helped at all. My dad had got me the mobile everyone was talking about on the news – the one with the battery problem – so it was turned off more than it was ever on.

"You wouldn't catch me in one of those places," belched Gary as he finished his pint and reached for a nearby glass of whisky. He was right – none of his family had bothered to visit my mum while she was on the intensive care ward, but I wasn't going to bring that up now. I just ignored him.

"Then, this last week, after she… went. Just waiting for the funeral. That's been the worst part. But now it's over I feel better."

"She was a good woman, your mum," said Gary, wincing as the whisky hit his throat. "Even if she did choose the wrong man to marry!" He laughed raucously, elbowing his wife in the ribs and spilling her drink. "There was another bloke sniffing round her when she first started seeing your dad. She ever tell you that? Norman, his name was. Went into the hotel business – made a fortune. More than your dad ever made, anyway."

I glanced over at my dad, his eyes red-rimmed as he chatted earnestly with one of my mum's Irish cousins. I felt the gnawing sensation begin to rise in my stomach again, but I forced it away.

Taking a deep breath, I attempted to continue my conversation with Mel. She's only a month younger than me so she was also approaching her exams, and I hoped the subject would provide a diversion from Uncle Gary's behaviour. I almost laughed. Things must be bad if I was choosing to talk about school.

"How are you?" I asked. "Got a lot of revision to do?"

"Course she has!" Gary interrupted before Mel could reply. "She's going to go on to college and university and do her family proud, aren't you sweetheart?" He grabbed his daughter and hugged her tightly.

Mel turned her face away from her dad's booze breath and nodded. "Yes, Dad," she mumbled. She offered me another piece of chewing gum, but I shook my head.

"Going to make something of herself, is our Melanie," continued Gary. "Get herself a proper, important job. She'll be the boss. Have a decent career. A future."

Mel did her best to remain cheerful. "I want to go into healthcare," she said to me.

"Yes, but at the top!" exclaimed Gary. "Hospital management, at least, not some poor lackey nurse mopping up other people's puke."

There it was again – that gnawing in my stomach.

"My mum was a nurse," I said through gritted teeth.

"Yeah, and look where that got her," said Gary, downing the rest of his whisky. "I tell you kid, nothing good comes from hanging around hospitals all day."

I'd swung the punch before I even knew it. There may not have been much of an aim to the strike, but there was plenty of force behind it. I hit the bottom of the whisky glass and rammed it hard into Gary's face. I heard the glass break – along with a couple of surgically-whitened teeth – and then the blood began to flow.

"You monster!" I yelled. "All those years my mum spent visiting you, and you never once came to see her. She was a brilliant nurse! She looked after thousands of people who needed her help, and then she got in her car and drove fifty miles to see you lot because she didn't want to lose touch with her family. The road goes in both directions, you know!"

By now, the pub was silent – all eyes on me. Gary had a hand clamped to his mouth, blood still spurting from between his fingers and running down over his clothes.

"Moron!" he glugged, spitting blood all over the table. "This shirt cost me more than your dead mother used to make in a week!"

I felt my fist clench as I readied myself for another attack, but a hand grabbed my shoulder and pulled me away from the table. I looked up through tear-filled eyes, expecting to see Ben beside me ready to give me an earful for spoiling the gathering, but it wasn't my brother who had pulled me away from Gary. It was the guy from the cemetery – the one who had been sitting on the mini digger.

When he spoke, he said something that would change my life forever…

"I can bring her back."

CHAPTER 2

CONTRACT

The man pushed me into a chair at a table near the back of the pub and sat opposite me. Smoothing down his blue work-overalls, he grabbed a small glass containing a sparkling, reddish drink and downed it in one go. Then he glared at me with dark eyes.

"You certainly know how to cause a scene."

I glanced over my shoulder to where my Aunt Anna was almost in tears; some of her husband's blood had spattered onto the white fur of her ridiculously expensive coat. "He deserved it," I grunted. "And a lot more besides."

"A lot of people deserve a lot of things," the man said.

I looked this weirdo up and down. What on earth was he talking about now? "Listen, mate," I said, starting to get up, "it's been a long and particularly rubbish day, so if you don't mind…"

The guy reached across the table and pushed me back into my seat. Then he grabbed his tiny glass and raised it to his lips again. That was odd. I could have sworn that glass was empty a few seconds ago.

"I'm Nick," he said, necking the auburn-coloured liquid. "And I meant what I said – I can bring your mum back…"

For the second time in five minutes, I felt my hand tighten into a fist. "You what?!"

Nick didn't shift his gaze. He stared me straight in the eyes as he pulled a piece of old, yellowing paper from inside his overalls and slid it across the table to me.

I glared right back at him – not wanting him to win our little staring contest – but I had to admit that I was also very intrigued by whatever might be written on that piece of paper. Eventually, I lowered my eyes and snatched it up.

It was a small sheet of paper, about the size of a page from a book, and it felt greasy against my fingers. The writing was tiny, scrawled in a flowing script in deep purple ink. I'd seen that sort of writing before. My dad collects old fountain pens – and this had almost certainly been written by something like that.

I was about to toss the paper back across the table when I noticed my mum's name near the top: Maria Emily Daniels. That caught my attention and I started to read. I couldn't understand all of the words – whoever had written this had eaten a dictionary for breakfast – but I got the gist of it.

All I had to do was sign my name at the bottom and my mum would come back from the dead.

No – that's not quite right. My mum would never have been dead in the first place.

"So…" said Nick, once I'd finished reading. "What do you think?"

I looked up at him. "What's the catch?"

Nick shrugged, then he downed another draught from his seemingly bottomless glass. "You just have to nominate someone to take her place," he said. "Someone to go into the coffin instead of her. One in, one out."

Behind me, I could hear Uncle Gary demanding loudly that my dad buy him a round of drinks to replace the ones I'd spilled.

"Where do I sign?"

Grinning, Nick pulled an ornate pen from a pocket in his overalls and handed it over. I filled in the nomination in bright scarlet ink, then held the nib over the line where I had to sign my name. I hesitated. What if it didn't work? Well, then – I guess I'd just wasted ten minutes chatting to some nutter in the corner of a pub. But, what if it *did* work…?

I signed my name.

There was a judder in the air around me – as though someone had just changed every TV channel across the entire world at the same time. Then I heard her voice.

"I can't believe he's gone at such a young age," said my mum.

It took me ages to gather up the courage to turn around but, when I did, there she was. My mum was sitting at the table – in the spot where Gary had been. Anna and Mel were with her, both dressed in black and their eyes red with tears.

It had worked!

I raced across the pub and flung my arms around my mum. "You're back!" I sobbed, burying my face in her shoulder.

"Back?" she said, lifting my head. "I only went to the toilet!"

I did my best to compose myself. "Yeah, right… it's just been, you know… an emotional day." I sat down next to her. She looked so well! Like the cancer had never even been near her.

"I think we're all still a little shocked," my mum said. "No one expected your Uncle Gary to go so quickly after his diagnosis."

Aunt Anna took a sip of her wine. The fur coat she was wearing – now black instead of white – looked even more expensive than the previous model. She certainly wasn't wasting any time in spending Uncle Gary's money.

"What about your exams?" my mum asked, taking Mel's hand in hers. "Will they give you extra time?"

"I… don't…" Mel stifled a sob and I suddenly felt a pang of regret for what I'd done. I'd sent an innocent man to his grave – well, a reasonably innocent man – just so I could have my mum back again. Was that right? Was that fair?

I pulled out the contract and held it beneath the table so the others couldn't see it. Maybe there was a way I could reverse my decision and nominate someone else – maybe someone at the hospital who was due to die anyway. Squinting, I tried to read the tiny scrawled script, but it was just too dark.

Then a flash of blue overalls caught my eye and I spotted Nick as he passed our table on his way out of the pub. "I'll be right back!" I said, jumping up to follow him.

The air was cold outside – colder than I'd expected. But there was no sign of Nick. He'd managed to vanish somehow. Maybe he'd had a taxi waiting. I pulled out my mobile and stared at the contract again, hoping there was a number I could call in the small print.

"What's that?" demanded a voice.

I spun round to find Mel standing behind me.

"What's what?"

"That piece of paper!" said Mel sternly. "I saw you reading it inside just now."

"It's… it's nothing," I lied. "Just something I found in the pub."

"Then why does it have my dad's name written on it?"

Blimey! She must have good eyesight!

"It doesn't!"

"Then you won't mind me having a look, will you?"

"It's private!"

"You said you'd just found it!"

Mel reached around my back and grabbed the contract in my hand. She pulled and I heard it begin to rip.

Then the channel changed again – and everything went black.

CHAPTER 3

DARKNESS

I was lying down and there was someone pressed up against me.

"Who's there?" I asked nervously.

"It's me, Mel… Where are we?"

"I don't know."

"What happened?"

"I don't know!"

We took a couple of moments to catch our breath. I could feel Mel's body pressed up against mine and I tried to wriggle back to make some space between us, but I couldn't move. "Hang on," I said. "I've got my mobile here…"

Wriggling around a little, I managed to pull my phone from my pocket and turn it on. The glow from the screen was enough to illuminate the tiny space around us. We were surrounded by soft, white silk – like the inside of a coffin.

Oh no!

I could feel Mel begin to panic. "No!" she breathed. "This can't be happening."

"Look, just calm down…"

"Calm down?" she cried. "We've been buried alive. Together!" She began to hammer on the lid of the coffin with her fists. "Help! HELP!"

"No one's going to hear us!" I snapped. "We're two metres underground!"

"But how?" asked Mel, her voice cracking. "Why?"

I sighed. No point keeping it a secret any more. So I told her what I'd done. I told her about Nick and how I'd nominated her dad on his contract.

"You idiot, Toby!" Mel screamed. "You've killed us both!"

"I didn't know this was going to happen, did I?"

"No – but you were happy enough when it was my dad in here!"

"Better him than my mum!"

We fell silent for a moment, both trying to catch our breath. It was getting stuffy and I realised with horror that we were running out of air. I didn't mention the fact, as I doubted it would have helped to lighten Mel's mood.

"Your mobile!" she cried. "We can call for help!"

"Brilliant!" I still had the phone in my hand, so I switched it on again and stared at the almost blinding light of the screen. *Please, please, please…*

My heart sank. "No signal," I said.

"There must be!"

"There isn't!"

"Keep trying!"

"I am! Where's your phone?"

"In my handbag, in the pub."

I stared in dismay at the two tiny words at the top of the screen: 'No service'. I got bad enough reception around here to begin with, so how I expected to get a signal underground was anybody's guess.

"Dial 999!" said Mel suddenly.

"I've told you, I haven't got a signal."

"You don't need one!" said Mel. "Emergency calls link directly to the police network, or another company's phone network – at least, I think they do. It's so you can get help wherever you are."

"I've never heard that," I admitted.

"It's got to be worth a try…"

She was right. With trembling fingers I began to dial. 9… 9… 9…

It started to ring!

"It's working!"

Mel grabbed my free hand and squeezed it tightly. "Yes!"

"Emergency, which service do you require?"

"Police!" I said. "My cousin and I are – "

The coffin fell dark. The light from the phone was gone.

"No! No, no, no!" I stabbed at the power button again and again. "NO!"

"What's wrong?" demanded Mel.

I fought back the urge to cry. "The battery's dead."

"You didn't charge it?"

"As much as I dared, yes. This is the model with the dodgy battery, remember."

We lay together in silence for a while, our breathing becoming increasingly laboured. I'm not sure how much time passed – I stopped wearing a watch ages ago and checked the time on my mobile if I needed to.

"They'll never find us, will they?" said Mel eventually.

"Of course they will," I said as reassuringly as possible, but I wasn't sure I believed my own words. "They'll be looking for us right now."

"Not if they think we're dead."

"They don't think that."

"I did, when you swapped your mum for my dad."

"That was different," I insisted.

"How?"

"I nominated your dad," I said, a pang of guilt gnawing at my stomach. "What happened to us was some sort of accident because we were fighting over the contract."

"Either way, they think we're dead," sighed Mel.

"They can't do!" I insisted. "They wouldn't bury both of us in the same coffin, for a start!"

"That's true!" said Mel. "You might be right – this wasn't meant to happen. Where's the contract?"

"In my pocket, I think. Why?"

"Take it out."

"What for? We won't be able to read it."

"Just do it!"

Wriggling around, I managed to get my hand into my other trouser pocket and pull out the sheet of paper. "Careful," I said to Mel as I handed it over. "It's starting to tear."

"I know," she said. "That's the bit I'm interested in."

I frowned in the darkness. "Why?"

"This only happened when we both grabbed the contract and it ripped."

"When you grabbed it!" I corrected her.

"All right, whatever! Either way – it might be the rip that caused this."

"So?"

"If we can fix the rip, maybe this will all reverse itself."

I thought about this for a moment. "That will mean your dad will be back in here instead of us."

"Not if you pull out of the contract. Get that bloke to cancel it."

"Then my mum will be in here."

Mel took a deep breath. "I know it's hard to accept, Toby – but your mum is dead. She had cancer for a long time, and now she's gone."

"No, she isn't," I spat. "We both saw her in the pub just before this happened."

"But she wasn't supposed to be there! You brought her back by messing around with this stuff – and look where that has got us…"

"OK," I said eventually. "So, what do we do?"

"I've already told you," said Mel. "We fix the contract."

"How?" I asked. "It may surprise you to hear this, but I left my roll of sticky tape and my stapler back in the pocket of my coat!"

"No need to be sarcastic!" said Mel. "Here… take this." She forced a small object into the palm of my hand.

"What is it?"

"Chewing gum," came the reply. "My last piece."

"Where did you get it?"

"There's a pocket in my dress."

"You've got a pocket in your dress and you don't keep your mobile phone in it?"

"Just shut up and chew, will you?!"

So I slid the piece of gum into my mouth and

started chewing.

"Do you have to do it so noisily?" Mel demanded. "It sounds like you're marching across a swamp."

"Stop moaning!" I barked. "I'm doing the best I can, it's just that – GLARK!"

"What's wrong?"

"I almost swallowed it."

"DON'T DO THAT! WE NEED IT!"

"I KNOW!"

I continued chewing for what seemed an age, but was probably only three or four minutes. The air was now incredibly stuffy and I was starting to feel drowsy. I didn't need my biology teacher to tell me that we were starting to feel the effects of carbon dioxide poisoning. If we stayed in this confined space for much longer, we'd both fall asleep and never wake up again.

"There!" I said, spitting the gum out into my hand. "Done."

"OK," said Mel. "Hand it over…"

I forced my hand down my side to hers and passed the lump of wet goo across.

"Yuck!" she moaned. "OK, I'm pressing it against the back of the contract and smoothing down the torn part so that the edges touch…"

The world shuddered again and we jumped as a neon-blue arc of lightning shot down from the sky and hit the black earth beside us with a deafening CRACK!

Mel and I slowly climbed to our feet and examined our surroundings. We were in some sort of desolate landscape in the midst of a storm. Ice-cold rain poured down over us, washing the dirt from the piles of bones and skulls that littered the ground at our feet. I stuffed the hastily repaired contract back into my pocket.

Then came the roar. Louder than the rain and sharper than the bolts of lightning that continued to pound the earth. We clamped our hands over our ears and watched in horror as what looked like a demon rose up from the soil, eyes blazing and gravestone-sized teeth gnashing together. It stomped towards us, hooves smashing the discarded bones into a fine, white powder that clung to the creature's leathery, red skin.

The demon considered us for a moment, then smiled.

It was then that I recognised the beast. I'd seen that smile before – only on a more human face.

This was Nick.

CHAPTER 4

ETERNITY

"Let us go!" Mel demanded. "We're here by mistake!"

Nick threw his head back and laughed. It sounded like the ground itself tearing apart. "Mistake?" he bellowed. "MISTAKE?! I don't make mistakes!"

"Maybe not," I said, trying to sound as brave as Mel had done. "But I did. I shouldn't have signed your stupid contract in the first place!"

Nick stooped to glare at me, fire dancing behind the dark pupils of his eyes. "And what do you expect me to do about that?" he thundered.

I shrugged. "Let us go?"

The demon rose up to its full height and laughed again. "You entertain me!" he roared. "Perhaps I shall keep you here to be my fool for all eternity!"

"Never!" I yelled.

Nick pointed a long-nailed finger in my direction. More blue lightning shot from the digit, hitting me in the chest and sending me flying back a few metres. Mel hurried over to check on me.

"Are you OK?" she asked, examining the scorch mark on my shirt.

"Never felt better," I grunted as she helped me to my feet. "I'm pretty sure I've got him worried now."

Taking a deep breath, I tried to summon up some courage – then I strode back over the carpet of human bones to face Nick again. "Very well!" I said. "I'll stay and entertain you – but I want you to let Mel go."

"No!" Mel cried, stumbling across a pile of skulls to stand beside me. She took hold of my hand and squeezed it tightly. "If Toby stays, then I stay too!"

Nick laughed again. "Two fools!" he cried. "Even better!"

"That's not the deal!" I shouted. Another bolt of blue electricity sent me sprawling.

Mel was beside me again in seconds. This time the burn mark was on the skin of my chest. "What are you doing?" she hissed. "You're making him angry!"

"That's the plan!"

"What?!"

"Just trust me!"

I staggered to my feet. "Nice shot!" I cried, staggering back towards the demon. "You should have a go at Mad Cats – you'd get the high score in no time!" I pulled my dead mobile phone from my pocket and held it up to the monster.

"Mad Cats?" spat the demon. "What nonsense is this?"

"It's not nonsense at all!" I insisted. "Mad Cats is the best-selling game for mobile phones ever. You see, these naughty dogs steal the cats' fish…"

"Silence!" Nick aimed another finger of lightning pain in my direction but, this time, I made sure my mobile phone was in the way. The blast of electricity surged into the device, instantly turning the phone red hot. I felt it burning my skin, but refused to let go.

"Hide!" I shouted to Mel.

"What?"

"Find somewhere to hide!"

Mel ducked behind a large, blackened boulder and watched as Nick's powerful lightning poured into my phone.

I gritted my teeth against the pain in my hand.

"You have to be careful, though!" I yelled. "You see, my dad doesn't know much about technology. He accidentally bought me the phone that was all over the news at the time due to a battery problem. Charge them too much and people found that they might… just… go… bang!"

I felt the phone begin to vibrate crazily in my hand and hurled it at Nick's feet. The mobile exploded, blasting up a shower of broken bones and rocks. The monster fell, clawing at its eyes with twisted fingers and screaming in agony.

The explosion threw me backwards. I hit the ground hard and risked a glance at my damaged hand. It was bleeding badly – just what I needed.

I pulled the demon's contract from my pocket and grabbed a shard of broken bone from the ground. Dipping the point in the blood from my palm, I scratched out the names I'd written on the piece of paper and replaced them with others – just as Nick clambered back to his cloven feet and stomped in my direction.

I stood and thrust the piece of paper out towards him. "You're too late!" I yelled.

Then the world shook one final time.

CHAPTER 5

AWAKE

I've been in the coffin – alone – for almost nine years now. And I've been awake for all that time. Turns out the drowsiness I'd felt when I was in here with Mel wasn't a lack of oxygen – just tiredness after a long and particularly rubbish day. No, I'm awake down here, all right. Properly awake. I occasionally fall into a restless sleep, but the dreams of being back up there don't last very long, and I do my best to ignore them.

And all because I'd signed my name on the wrong dotted line as Nick had pounded across the blackened, bone-strewn earth towards me. I didn't mean to; I'd planned to put everything back exactly the way it was before I'd had the fight with Uncle Gary – but I guess I panicked. I wrote the wrong name in the wrong place and accidentally condemned myself to – well, not death. This is much, much worse than death.

The good news is I'm able to move a bit more now that Mel's not crammed in here with me. Not that there's anything to do, of course.

I hear them come to visit from time to time – my mum and dad, my brother and sister, sometimes even Mel and Aunt Anna. Uncle Gary has yet to appear. At first, I screamed for help every time I realised someone was up there, leaving flowers – but no one ever seemed to hear me.

I'm glad – in a weird sort of way. I don't want to scare them – not after all they've been through (or, rather, think they've been through). To them, I've taken on my mum's story. I'm the one who suffered through the lengthy cancer treatment. I'm the one who lost my battle with the disease. They remember sitting around my hospital bed as the monitor readings began to fall. They remember holding my hands as I took that final, gasping breath.

I hope Uncle Gary didn't upset my mum at the get-together after my funeral.

Now and again, I wonder if Mel ever remembers the truth – even for a second or two. If she does, she never lets on when she visits on my birthday (I'm nearly twenty-four now!). Shame, really, as I have a favour to ask her. Nothing much – I just want to ask if she can find a way to get me a mobile phone down here.

I could really go for a game of Mad Cats to pass the time.

THE END